CW01498563

Reclaiming Robin Hood:
Folklore & South Yorkshire's Infamous Outlaw

Acknowledgements

Dr David Clarke, Ron Clayton, Dan Eaton,
Nigel Humberstone, Jo Wingate

With huge thanks to Pat Bailey, Anthony Bennett,
Martin Carter, Michael Eden, Rebecca Eyre,
Ashley Gregory, Dr Simon Heywood, Roseanne Hicks,
Robert Langham, Mike Pidd, Molly Williams

Illustrators: Lisa O'Hara, Anja Uhren, James Green, Tom J Newell
Book design: Ward 57
Cover illustration: Sarah Abbott
Maps © OpenStreetMap contributors

Contents

Introduction

ROBIN HOOD is firmly embedded in popular culture as one of the world's most well-known outlaws. Stretching back some 600 years, medieval ballads make mention of the infamous archer and the folklore no doubt reaches even further.

Naturally, like most storytelling however, the tales have evolved. Some of them have taken quite a departure from the earliest known documents. Robin Hood in the earliest ballads (from manuscripts dating back to around the mid 15th century) may have been fair-minded but he didn't rob from the rich to give to the poor; nor did he meet Maid Marian. He worshipped his beloved Virgin Mary and he frequented the forests and woodlands of Barnsdale and South Yorkshire.

We have looked into the South Yorkshire tales, trails and traditions behind the legend of Robin Hood, often referred to as Robin of Loxley. Our starting point for this booklet is a place that all the arrows point to as the birthplace of Robin of Loxley. Dan Eaton's detective work discovers what he believes to be the true location of Little Haggas Croft—the birthplace of Robin Hood.

An age-old debate around the legend of Robin Hood centres on whether he was a real medieval hero (largely debunked as a theory), a composite character or a popular figment of the imagination from many a fireside story. In Chapter Two Dr David Clarke takes us through some of the 'culprits' who may have inspired the ballads and folklore.

There are many figures who may have helped shape the stories told through the generations.

Loxley (the Hallamshire suburb in Sheffield) and a number of other locations across South and West Yorkshire and Derbyshire are also associated with these stories. Chapter Three sees a round up of some of the localities and lesser-known gems with links to Robin of Loxley including place names inspired by the legendary anti-hero and his outlaw associates. Who knows, you may find one of our 'silver arrow' plaques at some of the locations.

Barnsdale is the setting for one of the most pre-eminent early ballads, known as *The Gest of Robyn Hode* (gest meaning 'deeds' or 'acts'). Chapter Four features an extract from *The Gest* as published (in *South Yorkshire Folk Tales*) by Simon Heywood and Damien Barker. As Heywood and Barker mention, the full text consists of a "whopping 465 stanzas". The authors have given their interpretation of the ballads in prose. We have printed the first 'chapter' of the tale *The Poor Knight,* which gives some sense of why Robin may have been considered fair-minded and also depicts his devotion to the Virgin Mary.

One possible reason that the legend has evolved so much is that for decades Robin has been the darling of many a movie and TV series around the world and also a popular subject of video games since the early 1980s. Ashley Gregory, our aspiring writer (on an internship from Sheffield Hallam University) frames the features and the fiction in Chapter Five. How far have depictions departed from the first known written references—and what was the influence of writers and historians through the ages? Ashley considers the evolution of the characters, the historical setting and locations plus the key elements (including the music) that have combined to ensure the legend has endured.

The **Reclaiming Robin Hood** project led by Sensoria and partners has, in the last few years, celebrated the roots of South Yorkshire's outlaw via a film screening in Loxley Valley woodland (at Stoneface Creative) and an app of the locations relating to the Robin Hood legend.

The project is ongoing at the time of writing this accompanying booklet and future plans include silver arrow plaques at some of the locations mentioned plus an *Outlaw's Picnic* and a statue in Loxley.

Anthony Bennett's maquette of his proposed sculpture of a young Robin Hood.

All of the activities will keep alive the South Yorkshire connections with our fair-minded folklore outlaw.

overleaf
Woodcut with border 1503

1. The Riddle of Robin:
Finding the Birthplace of a Loxley Outlaw
Dan Eaton

Ask any audience attending a lecture on Robin Hood the following questions: to each there will be an entirely predictable answer.

Who has never read, heard or seen a tale of Robin Hood?
The answer is no-one.
Who has read the stories as an adult other than to children?
The answer is no-one.
Who has ever read the stories in the original versions?
The answer is no-one.

In one form or another, the tales have been told to children by adults who themselves learned them as children. That holds good for the last two hundred years, probably for much longer. It is thus that the legend has been transmitted and transmuted; and has endured.

Professor J.C. Holt, 1982

THE LEGEND OF ROBIN HOOD is perpetually evolving and, as Dr David Clarke discusses in Chapter Two, there are innumerable references to potential candidates in British history. There are, however, significantly fewer that bear import to his origins and this article uses specific references and records as a starting place to pinpoint the location of the birthplace of this key figure in local folklore.

Loxley became the first and foremost place associated with Robin's birth from over 400 years ago. Despite (at the time) being an under-populated and unheard-of rural backwater, in 1637 John Harrison left us with the tantalising clue of a specific reference as to where that location was according to oral traditions. Unfortunately, time has not been kind to local historians and the vast majority of the landscape Harrison observed was swept away over hundreds of years of enclosures, development and urbanisation leaving little trace in modern times. His original reference to Robin's birthplace of Little Haggas Croft (see below) has often been referenced in the area Normandale adjacent to Loxley (across the main road of Rodney Hill/Ben Lane that cuts through the two areas) because there are no obvious reference points to work from, but with new on-the-ground discoveries it seems that the people of Loxley might once again lay claim to the birthplace of Robin of Loxley (alias Robin Hood).

John Harrison and the Earl of Arundel and Surrey's survey

Throughout 1637 a surveyor, John Harrison, was employed by the wealthy and powerful Earl of Arundel & Surrey to establish a record of all his lands, possessions and rents due. Little is known of the personal life of Harrison, other than that he was not a local, but it is known that he was very methodical and meticulous in his recording noting sizes of parcels of land to within a few square feet, features of interest, and that this feat of documenting all the Earl's lands across Sheffield as far as Worksop took 43 weeks and three days to complete. When he reached Loxley he recorded specific plots of land, but the most significant was:

[verbatim quote]

230   Imprimis Great Haggas Croft (pasture) lying near Robin Hoods Bower & is invironed with Loxley ffirth & Cont.   .

231   Item *litttle Haggas Croft (pasture) wherein is ye foundacion of an house or Cottage where Robin Hood was borne* this piece is Compassed about with Loxley ffirth & Cont.   .   .   .   .   .

232   Item Bower wood lying betweene Loxley firth East & ye lands of Mr Eyre in part west & Cont.   .   .   .   .

| 233 | Item Bower field (arable) lying betweene ye last piece East & ye lands of Mr Eyre North & west & Loxley firth South & Cont. . . . . . |
| 220 | Hober Hill (pasture) lying betweene a way North east and Loxley firth on every side else & Cont. . . . |

There are a number of reasons for the 'lost location' of Little Haggas Croft but potentially the two most significant today are the uncertainty surrounding a westerly boundary between Common and 'Mr Eyre's lands', and the identity/location of Bower Wood and Field. Simplified and placed into a directional grid, Harrison's survey results read:

LOCATION	NORTH	SOUTH	EAST	WEST
Great Haggas Croft	Near Robin Hood's Bower*; surrounded by Loxley Firth†			
Little Haggas Croft	Surrounded by Loxley Firth†			
Bower Wood	Loxley Firth† (?)	Loxley Firth† (?)	Loxley Firth†	Mr Eyre's lands (part); Bower field (part)
Bower Field	Mr Eyre's lands (NW)	Loxley Firth†	Bower Wood	Mr Eyre's lands (NW)
Hober Hill (pasture) *Normandale*	'A way' (NE) *now Rodney Hill*	Loxley Firth†	'A way' (NE) *now Rodney Hill*	Loxley Firth†

* Suggested by Dr Clarke as being a part of Bower Field/Wood.

† Firth is the 17th century term denoting Common lands, not owned by any one given individual.

to Loxley Edge

LOXLEY COMMON
merging into Bower Wood

BOWER PLANTATION/WOOD

Bland Lane

Bower
Cottage

Field boundary
removed c.1900—
Mr Eyre's land

**BOWER
FIELD**

Possible
site of
Robin Hood's
Bower

Post-17th century field,
most likely common
land in 1637

Area of established
holly and possible site
of Haggas Croft

● Boundary Stone—denoting westerly edge
of former common land

**ROBIN
WOOD**

Rodney
Hill Allotments

Former Common land
(pre-enclosure)

Phillips Road

Archer Gate

Lee Road

Phillips Road

South View Rise

South View Close

Rodney Hill

Rodney Hill

Rodney
Hill/Woodstock
Road

France Road

Chase Road

Chase
Road/France
Road

Occupation Lane

Loxley Primary
School

Chase Road

Rodney Hill—
previously known
as Hober Hill

Rodney
Hill/South
View Rise

Cavendish Ave

LOXLEY

Rodney Hill

Rodney
Hill/Chase
Road

Rodney Hill

NORMANDALE
site of Hober Hill pasture

Austin Court

Woodstock Road

Rodney Hill

Rodney
Hill/Loxley
Road

Normandale Avenue

Auckland Avenue

Austin Close

Keswick Close

The Grove

The Grove

**Continuation of Common land
to lower fields above
Loxley River**

Loxley Road

Chase Farm

100m
300ft

B6077

Loxley
Road/Black
Lane/Cemetery

Loxley
Road/The
Grove

Loxley Road

Loxley Road

Loxley Road

The identity of these areas has never been successfully achieved in modern times however on 19th century O.S. maps a substantial area to the north of Rodney Hill, between the modern allotments and Loxley Common, is listed as 'Bower Plantation'. When this is used as a starting point, pieces of the puzzle begin to fall into place. Just to the west of the Bower plantation is a field, still in existence today, that bears all the hallmarks of 'assarting', i.e. a very early agricultural area cleared from woodland during the Middle Ages (as opposed to the 17th–18th century as many in Loxley are, and would have come into being after 1637). It is irregularly shaped, isolated within woodland and most importantly directly where it should be in terms of Harrison's notes.

The second feature previously left unidentified was the westerly edge of Loxley Common that Bower Field/Wood abutted; in the area now known as Robin Wood and owned by Loxley Primary School lies a roughly hewn stone, approximately 4 feet high by 1.5 feet wide with a cross carved in its centre *(see image, page 34)*. This, it can be suggested, was one of the original boundary markers to denote the edge of Loxley Common and appears to be of great age; by following the still existing stone walls today it is clear that it continues to provide a straight line approximately parallel to Loxley Edge and travels for well over a mile to the north-west. It is clear from all O.S. maps produced that this boundary pre-dates all others as every other wall joins it rather than interrupts it.

These two features provide a piecemeal description of where Harrison was looking nearly four hundred years ago; the next step is to try to identify the Haggas Crofts themselves.

Given the order that Harrison explored and recorded these areas it is proposed that he began at 'the way' [road] on Hober Hill (now Rodney Hill) and travelled north to reach the Haggas Crofts before Bower Wood/Field, meaning he would have to pass through the area between the road and field today. Approximately 25 metres to the east of the previously mentioned boundary stone is an area that over many years has been in between shifting boundaries and as a consequence left undisturbed.

It is only small, approximately 20 metres square, but is densely populated with ancient and well-established holly trees with virtually no other foliage present. In the middle ages and through to the mid-18th century coppiced and pollarded (maintained/managed) holly was used as animal fodder throughout the winter. In 1696, Yorkshire antiquarian Abraham de la Pryme stated:

> In the south west of Yorkshire, at and about Bradfield ... they feed all their sheep in winter with holly leaves and bark, which they eat more greedily than any grass. To every farm there is many holly trees ... and all these holly trees are smooth leaved and not prickly. As soon as the sheep sees the sheppard come with the ax in his hand they all follow him to the first tree he comes at, and stands all round about the tree, expecting patiently the fall of the bow, which, when it is falln, all as many as can eats thereof, and the sheppard going further to another tree, all those that could not come in unto the eating of the first follow him to this, and so on. As soon as they have eaten all the leaves they begin of the bark and pairs it all off.

The local name for these areas were Haggs, Haggas' or Hollins, and hence Little and Great Haggas Croft. This area, it can be argued is the probable site of Great Haggas Croft, due to its proximity to Bower Field, presence of many old holly trees, and sheer probability in comparison to the minute size of Little Haggas Croft (a mere 0.6 acres, compared to Great Haggas Croft's 2.29 acres) but it could not be entirely discounted as being the birthplace of Robin of Loxley in Little Haggas Croft. Little Haggas Croft could also have potentially been somewhere between this point and Bower Wood to the north-east, but certainly not more than a few hundred metres away.

Despite the improbability of unequivocally identifying *the* Robin of Loxley (although Dr Clarke puts forward several potential contenders), it can be said that the remains of the holly croft in Robin Wood holds up to scrutiny as one of the locations visited by John Harrison in 1637, and where he made first note of a direct birthplace for a local folklore hero turned global phenomenon. There remains an atmosphere and intensity to the place should you visit, and the knowledge that the people of Loxley had claimed this place as the birthplace of a national treasure through their own oral traditions makes it even more special to those of us who remain proudly associated to it today.

Dan Eaton
Loxley Primary School

overleaf
Robin Hood ILLUSTRATION BY LISA O'HARA

2. Figures Forming Folklore:
the Many Historical Figures that may have helped form the Legend of Robin Hood
Dr David Clarke

We don't need convincing.
We know Robin Hood was from Loxley.

John Robinson, quoted in the Sheffield Telegraph, 23 June 2016.

STORIES ABOUT AN OUTLAW who robbed the rich and gave to the poor have been popular since at least the 13th century. Today most people associate Robin Hood and his Merry Men with Sherwood Forest and Nottingham, but this is a relatively modern tradition. The early ballads locate the stories in the area between Wakefield and Doncaster in present-day Yorkshire. This area was notorious during the Middle Ages as a haunt of highway robbers and thieves.

Robin Hood is one of the most enduring of England's folk heroes. But there is no unequivocal documentary reference to the Robin Hood of the ballads and the historical sources that do mention him are jumbled up with invented history and folklore. What is not in any doubt is the popularity of the legend with the ordinary folk.

The earliest documentary reference to him appears in Langland's *Piers Plowman* (circa 1377) where a character says he is familiar with the 'rhymes of Robin Hood'. Robin's exploits are the subject of 38 ballads; the earliest *Lyttell Geste of Robyn Hode* dates from 1450.

In the ballads he is portrayed as an outlawed yeoman who is constantly at odds with authority and a sworn enemy of the rich and powerful including his nemesis, the Sheriff of Nottingham. But contrary to the contemporary legend that Robin robbed the rich and gave to the poor, in the ballads he keeps his treasure for himself.

The tradition that Robin Hood was born in Sheffield can be traced back more than 500 years in documentary sources and even further in the oral tradition. The people of Hallamshire—

the old name for the Sheffield district—were makers of weapons and the symbol of the city is the Sheaf of Arrows. An ancient carving showing an archer hunting in a dense forest decorates the Anglo-Saxon cross shaft that once stood outside Sheffield's parish church, now the Cathedral. The stone, dated to 850, was found in Sheffield Park, one of the greatest hunting parks in medieval England. According to local legend, Robin once fired an arrow from beneath a tree in the Park that stuck fast in the door of the parish church!

The earliest sources are consistent that Robin's birthplace was in the tiny hamlet of Loxley, in Hallamshire (a modern suburb of Sheffield). Loxley or Loc's lea in the parish of Bradfield is first mentioned as a place name in 1329. The ancient manor of Wadsley adjoined Loxley Chase and lay within a huge forest that stretched from the Peak District into present–day Nottinghamshire, long before the modern county boundaries were established.

Some Early References

In 1382 a Robert Dore of Wadsley, also known as Robert Hode, appears in Patent Rolls as having received a pardon from King Richard II. Dore is listed alongside two other men who took up arms to eject the hated Mayor of York, John Gisburne, following a peasants' revolt in the city. Sir Guy of Gisborne appears as a mortal enemy of Robin Hood in one early ballad, dated from 1475. Although it is tempting to make a link between the pardon and the ballad, there is no other evidence available, but this story could easily have 'fed into' local folklore. Another Robert Hode is listed among the Freemen of York in 1391 but, again, we cannot be sure if he was the same man because the nick-name Robert (or Robin) Hood was adopted by many individuals during the early middle ages for a variety of purposes. Robyn or Robert and Hood were all common names in the medieval period and turn up frequently in parish records and court rolls. For example, a Pipe Roll from 1226 mentions 'Robin Hood, a fugitive' in Yorkshire and the Poll Tax Rolls from 1379 list a Robert Hode living in Handsworth, Sheffield, with his wife Agnes. The historian Joseph Hunter also found a late Elizabethan reference to a forester known as Robin Hood Bright who was a member of the ancient family resident at Whirlow Hall in the parish of Ecclesall two centuries later.

Joseph Hunter and Robin Hood

Sheffield-born Hunter was assistant keeper of the Public Records Office for three decades until his death in 1861. He had privileged access to medieval documents as he carefully built his own theory about the true identity of the yeoman outlaw. His research found references to a Robert Hood and his wife Matilda in the court rolls of Wakefield, 1316-17, during the reign of King Edward II (1307–27). He also found a slightly later reference in royal accounts of payments made to a porter called Robert or Robyn Hood in 1324.

Hunter decided these were the same man and went on to propose this Robin had joined the rebel army that supported the Earl of Lancaster, the King's cousin, who was defeated at the Battle of Boroughbridge in 1322 and executed. Hunter searched the ballads for corroboration and was convinced he found it in the *Lyttell Geste*. A poetic section of the ballad refers to a visit made by 'our comely king' Edward to the greenwood where he meets and pardons Robin Hood. The royal records confirmed that Edward II had indeed travelled through Yorkshire and Lancashire to the city of Nottingham in 1323.

Joseph Hunter believed he had identified *the* Robin Hood. Writing in 1852 he said this theory 'appears to me to be, in all likelihood, the outline of his life' but he had to concede the evidence was entirely circumstantial and, in fact, 'there were many Robin Hoods'.

There is, in fact, no evidence the two Robin Hoods he identified were the same person or that anyone of that name had fought at Boroughbridge. Professor Sir James Holt, in *Robin Hood* (1982), said the only hard evidence was the record of the king's visit to Nottingham. All the other details were a 'hypothetical reconstruction' that could be easily demolished. But the caution urged by historians has done nothing to dissuade legions of other writers from taking Hunter's theory as the gospel truth. Even Professor Holt had to admit that Hunter may have been wrong about the detail but was looking in the right place for evidence—in Yorkshire. In the earliest records, Sherwood is only mentioned in passing but Nottingham's sheriff does appear as Robin's adversary. This explains how the scene of the action shifted in later centuries from Barnsdale, near Doncaster, to the now more familiar Sherwood Forest and Nottingham.

All we can say for sure today is the surname Hood was a nickname given to, and adopted by, assorted felons and outlaws as early as the 13th century. Furthermore, there is some evidence that a man or men who called themselves Robin Hood lived in this part of southwest Yorkshire at some point from this time until the 16th century. What we cannot say for sure is this was the Robin Hood of the Hollywood legends that we are familiar with today. The medieval sources all refer to a Robin (or Robyn) Hood as a highwayman who was active in the area northwest of Doncaster known as Barnsdale Bar. In the middle ages this was a wild and dangerous region that stretched across what is present-day South Yorkshire from Doncaster south/southwest towards Loxley, Rivelin and Sherwood. The geographical link is strengthened by the number of Robin Hood and Little John place-names concentrated in this area of Yorkshire and in north Derbyshire (see *Locations Relating to the Legend of Robin Hood*). A grave said to be that of Robin's faithful lieutenant Little John has been pointed out to visitors in Hathersage churchyard since at least the mid-17th century. Some of these place-names may be recent and others may relate to older, oral traditions.

Robin Hood's Bower at Loxley

In the folklore of Hallamshire, Robin is also known as Robin of Loxley or Robert Locksley. In 1795 Joseph Ritson published a collection of the ballads in which he declared: 'Robin Hood was born at Locksley in the county of Nottingham'. To confuse matters further, in Sir Walter Scott's novel *Ivanhoe* (1820) 'Locksley' is the title of Robin Hood's character, portrayed as a Saxon yeoman (though it is hinted he is of a more noble birth). He is leader of a band of outlaws who help rescue several 'high ranking' Saxons held captive by Norman knights.

There are Loxleys in Warwickshire and Staffordshire but the village on the Sheffield river valley of the same name, has the earliest links to the legend. Joseph Hunter, in his history of *Hallamshire* (1819) referred to the Loxley valley as having 'the fairest pretensions to be the Locksley of the old ballads'. One of the earliest references to Loxley appears in a prose life of Robin Hood that forms part of a Sloane manuscript, dating from the early 17th century. This is a collection of notes made by a respected antiquarian, Roger Dodsworth, who may have had access to primary sources some of which have not survived. Drawing upon evidence from two named sources, he writes that:

> Robert Locksley, born in Bradfield parish, in Hallamshire, wounded his stepfather to death at plough: fled into the woods, and was relieved by his mother until he was discovered. Then he came to Clifton-upon-Calder, and came acquainted with Little John who kept the kine.

Professor Holt did not place much reliance upon the Sloane MS but Dodsworth's note does link this isolated hamlet, hardly known outside the parish of Sheffield, with the folk hero and, as Dan Eaton explored in the first chapter, it has corroboration from another surprising source. In 1637 the Duke of Norfolk, lord of Sheffield Manor, commissioned John Harrison to complete a detailed survey of his lands that surrounded the medieval castle. When he reached Loxley, Harrison visited an area of pasture at Great Haggas Croft 'lying near Robin Hood's Bower'. The very next item in his itinerary mentions Little Haggas Croft wherein he was shown the foundations of a 'house or cottage where Robin Hood was born', surrounded by the greenwood of Rivelin forest. He then refers to a Bower wood and a Bower field. Drawing upon Harrison's survey, Sheffield folklorist Sidney Addy identified Robin Hood's Bower as a semi-permanent building, likely to have been a large enclosure that was constructed in the forest every summer. Here local people played the part of Robin Hood or the King of the May, Little John and Maid Marian in the annual 'summer game' that Addy compared to the Castleton Garland ceremony that takes place in Derbyshire every May. This custom was not unique to Loxley. There are churchwardens' accounts of similar bowers elsewhere in England, sometimes in churchyards as at nearby Ecclesfield, where it was called the Summer Hall in the 18th century. There was no church at Loxley so the structure must have been built in the heart of the forest and, as the Harrison survey suggests, this was a more permanent structure than a tent.

In his book *Hallamshire* Hunter says the remains of a house at Loxley 'in which it was pretended he [Robin] was born were formerly pointed out' were visible in the late 18th century. In a letter published by the Sheffield Telegraph in 1931, Willis Crookes, then owner of the farmhouse at Normandale, said his father remembered seeing the ruins as a boy but they were removed in 1834. The octogenarian Crookes said the local tradition was that Robin and his stepfather were working on some land near Loxley Chase Farm when they had a violent argument 'and Robin Hood cut down his step-father with his scythe and killed him'. After he was outlawed, Robin hid in a cave on the chase and was provided for by his mother until he fled to the West Riding where he met Little John and Much the Miller's son. This strong oral tradition persisted in the Loxley valley three centuries after Harrison's visit but attempts by historians to identify a named Robert or Robin Hood in Sheffield's manorial records have been unsuccessful.

In the second edition of *The Truth About Robin Hood* (1973) P. Valentine Harris refers to research by Mr F. Loxley Preston of Sheffield who found a reference in the lay Subsidy Rolls of a Thomas de Lokeslay and his son Adam who held land in Bradfield parish in 1378–79:

> Some court rolls have survived from 1275 but Robert Locksley is not recorded … He may have been a younger son of Thomas or, if he lived at a later date, a younger, and therefore landless, son, whose name would not necessarily appear in the manorial records.

In making these inferences Mr Preston was in danger of falling into the same trap as Joseph Hunter. The lack of clear historical evidence led some writers to reject the entire idea that Robin was a real person. In more recent years he has been 'identified' as Robin Wood, Robin Goodfellow and The Green Man, all pagan spirits of the greenwood. In 1888 Norton-born folklorist Sidney Addy said it was not necessary to consider if Robin Hood was born in Nottinghamshire or Hallamshire 'for he never lived in the flesh … he belongs to mythology and romance, not to history'. But he felt the story recorded in 1637 could not have been invented by John Harrison, and 'he must have heard it from the lips of men who then occupied that secluded village, and probably the belief had long been current that some man of prowess had once inhabited these wilds, had stolen the king's deer, and accomplished feats of bravery and generosity'. He added:

> … when riding on a coach in Scotland, hearing the coachman, as we passed by a ruined cottage, say: "Gentlemen, this is one of the houses where Rob Roy was born". And here we have learnt on a much earlier authority that Bradfield was one of the places where "Robin Hood" was born.

Robin Hood: Earl of Huntingdon

As we have seen, there have been many attempts to identify a 'real' Robin Hood but none are completely convincing. Joseph Hunter was not the first or last authority to construct an imagined genealogy for the folk hero. The Sloane manuscript claims that Robin was born in 1160 and died in 1247 at Kirklees Priory and this invented history was widely adopted by Elizabethan storytellers who revived the legend for a new audience. The epitaph on Robin Hood's Grave in Kirklees Park, West Yorkshire, dismissed by Hunter as 'a fabrication', reads:

> Here underneath this little stone lies Robert, Earl of Huntingdon
> No archer was as he so good and people called him Robin Hood
> Such outlaws as he and his men will England never see again.

The idea that Robin was an impoverished or disinherited earl first appears in a series of plays by Richard Grafton and Anthony Munday during the 16th century. Before that time Robin Hood was always described as a yeoman and was never described as being of noble birth. But in *The Downfall of Robert Earl of Huntingdon* the legend is shifted backwards to the reign of Richard I (the Lionheart) and Munday invents a love triangle between Robin, Maid Marian and the wicked King John. The reign of Richard I was adopted by Sir Walter Scott as the historical setting for his hugely influential novel *Ivanhoe* published in 1820.

But there is one more twist in the tale. The noble title Earl of Huntingdon was one of several bestowed by William the Conqueror upon the last Saxon lord of Hallamshire, Earl Waltheof, in the aftermath of the Norman conquest. Born in the mid-eleventh century, Waltheof is a local hero much like Robin Hood, who rebelled against the Conqueror and was executed in 1076. He was the son of Siward, the Danish Earl of Northumbria who led the armies of King Edward the Confessor against Macbeth. In some 19th century texts the Saxon lords of Hallamshire are described as descendants of the early medieval kings of Scotland through the marriage of Waltheof's daughter Maud to David, King of Scotland, in 1113. Therefore, the last two Earls of Huntingdon were part Scottish and part Norman. This fact became a source of embarrassment for Victorian writers who sought evidence in support of *Ivanhoe*'s romanticised depiction of the yeoman in good company with Saxon nobles and freedom fighters.

It was a short journey from here for the legend of Robin Hood to become entwined with that of Earl Waltheof. He was a real historical figure who really did rebel against the Normans and paid with his life. Both Robin and Waltheof have been at various times—in both fiction and factual accounts—portrayed as Saxon freedom fighters. The most influential source for this idea is *Ivanhoe*, published one year before Hunter's history of *Hallamshire*. Scott set his novel in 12th century South Yorkshire, during the reign of King Richard. It portrays an invented, ongoing conflict between the Saxons and their Norman lords. Many subsequent film and TV interpretations of the Robin Hood legend have plots based around the stories invented by the Elizabethans that were given new life by Sir Walter Scott.

Fact or fiction, Robin Hood and his merry men continue to appear in plays, novels, children's books, cinema, TV programmes and comic books. The character of the folk hero and those of his companions have become such a fundamental part of English identity and folklore that we take the story of 'Robin of Sherwood' for granted. But the truth, as we have seen, is much more complex. What we can say for sure is that he, or someone who called himself by that name, was born at Loxley in the modern city of Sheffield and consistent folk tales have been embedded in the area for centuries. The Yorkshire connection has always been there and the moniker 'Robin of Loxley' has since become rooted in popular culture in the form of countless books, plays, films and TV programmes.

Dr David Clarke
Associate Professor,
Centre of Culture, Media and Society, Sheffield Hallam University

Please see page 41 for further reading references.

A1

Barnsley

Doncaster

Consibrough

Rotherham

Loxley

Sheffield

Hathersage

the
PEAK
DISTRICT

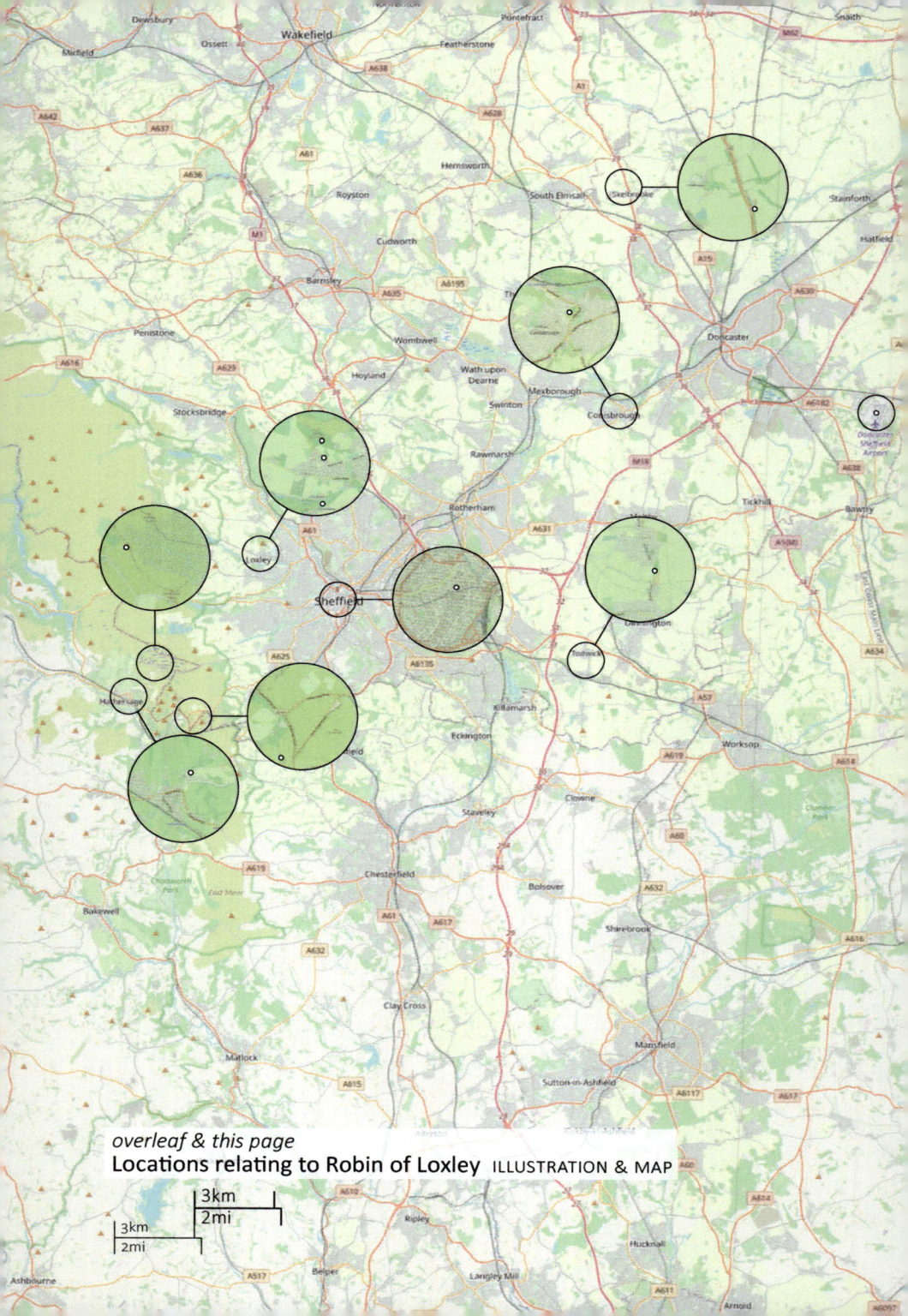

overleaf & this page
Locations relating to Robin of Loxley ILLUSTRATION & MAP

3km
2mi

3km
2mi

3. Locations Relating to the Legend of Robin Hood
Dr David Clarke

DR DAVID CLARKE has chosen just some of the localities with links to Robin of Loxley including place names inspired by the legendary anti-hero and his outlaw associates. The list starts with Loxley and Sheffield and moves to other areas around South Yorkshire (including around Rotherham and Doncaster) and then on to locations in Derbyshire. You may find one of our 'silver arrow' plaques at some of the locations.

Little Haggas Croft, Loxley
OS REFERENCE: SK 31128 90217

For some time it was thought that the site of Little Haggas Croft, the birthplace of Robin of Loxley, was located on Rodney Hill where Normandale House now stands. The foundations of the house survived until the Victorian era. The tradition was noted in a survey of the manor in 1637 and was still current in the area early in the 20th century. The ruins were visible until 1834.

According to a note in the Sloan manuscript of 1620, Robin killed his stepfather in the fields and fled into the woods at Rivelin. The 1637 survey also refers to 'Robin Hoods Bower' in Rivelin firth (forest). The bower may have been a tent or structure that was used for the annual Summer Games.

However as mentioned in Chapter One, Dan Eaton puts forward another location in the area now known as 'Robin Wood'. On this site, owned by Loxley Primary School, lies a roughly hewn stone, with a cross carved in its centre (see photograph). Dan suggests this was one of the original boundary markers denoting the edge of Loxley Common—

it appears to be of great age and this boundary pre-dates all others (see pages 15–16).

Approximately 25 metres to the east of the boundary stone is an area that has largely been left undisturbed. It is small, approximately twenty metres square, and densely populated with well-established holly trees. This area is a possible site of Great Haggas Croft, due to its proximity to Bower Field, presence of many old holly trees, and sheer probability in comparison to the minute size of Little Haggas Croft but it could not be entirely discounted as being the birthplace of Robin of Loxley in Little Haggas Croft. Dan also proposes that Little Haggas Croft could also have potentially been somewhere between this point and Bower Wood to the north-east, but certainly not more than a few hundred metres away.

Robin Hood's Well, Loxley
OS REFERENCE: SK 31134 89342

This natural spring was described by Joseph Hunter as 'a well of fine clear water' rising near the bed of the River Loxley. It can be found a short distance along the footpath behind the former Robin Hood and Little John pub in the area known as Little Matlock Wood. Other wells and springs named after Robin Hood can be found in Low Hall Wood at Burncross in Sheffield, on the Longshaw Estate and on the Howden Moors near Bradfield.

Robin Hood's Cave, Loxley

This rough cave or shelter on Wadsley Common/Loxley Edge was identified in local folklore as the place where Robin hid after he was outlawed. The location was known as Cave House and nearby was a rock trough that reputedly supplied water to his hideout. The cave was demolished during the 1920s and is also mentioned in a 19th century ghost story as the hiding place of a murderer.

Sheffield Cathedral

OS REFERENCE: SK 35399 87507

A legend recorded in the 19th century by Sidney Addy tells of a thorn tree in Sheffield under which Robin Hood once took shelter. From here he fired an arrow that stuck fast in the church door at Sheffield, one mile away! In the modern cathedral the Sheaf of Arrows, the symbol of the city, can be seen in the Chapel of St George. Arrows were made by medieval metalworkers in the town. The symbol also appears above the head of Waltheof, the last Saxon Earl of Hallamshire, in the stained glass window dedicated to the Six Worthies. In some later versions of his legend, Robin is a disinherited nobleman, the Earl of Huntington. This was one of the titles bestowed upon Earl Waltheof after the Norman conquest of England and some Victorian authors claimed Robin was a direct descendant of the Saxon rebel. Waltheof was executed in 1076 after he was drawn into a plot against the conqueror.

Robin Hood's Trysting Tree, Kiveton Park, Todwick, Rotherham

OS REFERENCE: SK 49751 83799

> Signed by us upon the eve of St Withold's day, under the great trysting oak in the Harthill-walk,

In his 1820 novel *Ivanhoe*, Sir Walter Scott refers to the 'great trysting tree' that was used a meeting place by Robin Hood. The original tree blew down in a storm and was replaced by the Duke of Leeds at

the beginning of the 20th century by a sapling grown from an acorn taken from the Major Oak. This tree stood at the edge of the 'Bluebell Wood' at Kiveton Hall Farm until 1973 when it was cut down during road widening. A third oak was planted and today this is used by the Kiveton Park Folk Club as a place to meet and dance at dusk every May Eve. The plaque reads:

On this site once stood Robin Hood's Trysting Tree immortalised in Sir Walter Scott's novel Ivanhoe. It was replaced in 1901 by a sapling of the Major Oak, planted by the Duke of Leeds. This plaque was erected to celebrate the planting of its successor by Kiveton Park Folk Club and was commemorated by Gerard F Young Esq. the Lord Lieutenant of South Yorkshire on the 18th May 1974.

The replacement tree and plaque can be found in woodland directly opposite the town's coat of arms at the southern entrance to Todwick.

Robin Hood's Well, Doncaster
OS REFERENCE: SE 51901 11755

Alongside the A1 at Skelbrooke, six miles northwest of Doncaster. Joseph Hunter considered this one of the earliest place-names that links the outlaw with Barnsdale, a notorious haunt of highwaymen and robbers. It was described as 'Robin Hood's Stone' in 1422 and was situated close to Ermine Street, the Great North Road, and was a natural halting place for travellers who would stop at the well to take refreshment. All that remains today is an 18th century stone folly that has been moved to a position in a layby beside the busy A1.

Doncaster Sheffield Airport (previously Robin Hood Airport)

OS REFERENCE: SK 66062 98202

The former RAF Finningley airbase sits on the boundary between Yorkshire and Nottinghamshire. During the Cold War it was used as a base for nuclear-armed V-bombers. It was decommissioned in 1996 and reopened as an international airport for civil aviation in 2005. A bronze statue of Robin Hood by Neale Andrew was installed in the first floor passenger terminal at the opening attended by South Yorkshire actors Sean Bean and Brian Blessed. The use of the outlaw's name in the title of the airport caused some controversy at the time. The airport is now marketed under the 'Doncaster Sheffield' branding.

Conisbrough Castle

OS REFERENCE: SK 51468 98909

Located north-east of Conisbrough town centre (off the A630) and south-west of Doncaster. Conisbrough Castle inspired Sir Walter Scott's novel *Ivanhoe* published 1820. Scott made Conisbrough Castle the residence of the Saxon noble Athelstane in his highly romanticised historical novel that also features Locksley as an outlaw yeoman.

> The outlaw's [sic. Robin Hood's] opinion proved true; and the King, attended by Ivanhoe, Gurth and Wamba, arrived, without any interruption, within view of the Castle of Coningsburgh, while the sun was yet in the horizon.
>
> There are few more beautiful or striking scenes in England, than are presented by the vicinity of this ancient Saxon fortress. The soft and gentle river Don sweeps through an amphitheatre, in which cultivation is richly blended with woodland, and on a mount, ascending from the river, well defended by walls and ditches, rises this ancient edifice, which as its Saxon name implies was, previous to the Conquest, a royal residence of the kings of England.
>
> *Ivanhoe, Walter Scott 1820*

Little John's Well, Longshaw Estate, near Hathersage, Derbyshire

OS REFERENCE: SK 2657 7946

A flight of worn rustic stone steps leads down from the Wooden Pole, Longshaw footpath (Wooden Pole Car Park is off the A625). At the bottom is a stone trough with water that rises from a natural spring. The National Trust states:

[Little John's] 'well' probably originated as a watering place for stock travelling along the old road, as was Robin Hood's Well. Or it could have been created in the 19th century as a parkland 'romantic feature', built to complement Robin Hood's Well and may have figured in earlier folklore ... No excavations or surveys have been carried out. This feature is also known as feature 33 in Barnatts Survey, 1994.

Robin Hood's Cave, Stanage Edge, Derbyshire

OS REFERENCE: SK 244 836

This well-known cave is marked on the O.S. map. It lies on the county boundary between South Yorkshire and Derbyshire. The cave has two entrances and has been used as shelter, lookout and dwelling place since the Ice Age. Today it is popular with rock climbers and can be found and entered from the footpath above the edge. The place-name link with the outlaw is recent as the cave is called Sled House on 17th century maps. It was first described as Robin Hood's Cave in 1868.

Little John's Grave, Hathersage, Derbyshire

OS REFERENCE: SK 23407 81832

Eight miles south of Loxley in St Michael's churchyard, surrounded by railings and sheltered by yew trees, is what is said to be the last resting place of Robin Hood's faithful lieutenant. In a manuscript note from 1617 Elias Ashmole states:

> Little John lyes buried in Hatherseech Church yard within 3 miles fro [Castleton] in High Peake with onre Stone set up at his head and another at his Feete, but a large distance between them.

Ashmole refers to 'part of his bow' at that time hanging up inside the church. Tradition has it that after burying his master in Kirklees, Little John returned to his Derbyshire home where he spent his last days in an old cottage to the east of the churchyard. In 1847 its occupant, Jenny Shard, said the tradition had been handed down through her family. The cottage was demolished in the late 19th century and the current 'gravestone', in the care of the Ancient Order of Foresters, is recent.

An older stone, marked *JL*, in the church porch is often mentioned as the original headstone.

The grave itself was opened in 1784 and a large thighbone was found that was, for some time, on display in the village. For many years Little John's bow, cap, arrows and chain mail were kept in the church but the bow was moved by the village squire to Cannon Hall near Barnsley. It is possible these were used by villagers who played the role of outlaws in the annual Summer Games. S.O. Addy suggested the stones originally functioned as the village perch, a standard length of measure in the middle ages. This was thirteen feet in length, exactly that marked by the distance between the two stones that marked the head and foot of the 'grave'.

Dr David Clarke
Associate Professor,
Centre of Culture, Media and Society, Sheffield Hallam University

with contributions from
Jo Wingate & Nigel Humberstone
Sensoria

FURTHER READING:

S.O. Addy. (1888). *A Glossary of Words used in the neighbourhood of Sheffield.* English Dialect Society.

S.O. Addy. (1924). *Robin Hood's Bower at Loxley.* Proceedings of the Hunter Archaeological Society vol 2.

P. Valentine Harris. (1973). *The Truth About Robin Hood.* Linneys of Mansfield.

Simon Heywood. (2015). *South Yorkshire Folk Tales.* The History Press.

James Holt. (1982). *Robin Hood.* Thames & Hudson.

Joseph Hunter. (1819). *Hallamshire.*

Joseph Hunter. (1852). *The Great Hero of Ancient Minstrelsy.* London.

W.R. Mitchell. (1978). *Exploring the Robin Hood Country.* Dalesman.

Sir Walter Scott. (1820). *Ivanhoe.*

Simpson, Jacqueline and Roud, Steve. (2000). *A Dictionary of English Folklore.* Oxford University Press.

overleaf
Robin Hood ILLUSTRATION BY ANJA UHREN

4. extract from
The Gest of Robin Hood—The Poor Knight
From *South Yorkshire Folk Tales*
by Simon Heywood & Damien Barker

When Robert Hood of Loxley was outlawed— as people had often said he would be, and they were sad as they said it, for Robin was a good lad, well liked in Loxley for his blue eyes and his winning ways, and an outlaw's life was generally hard and short— he fled at once to the wastes of Barnsdale. His parting shot was to say that he would obey the king's law when the king himself came to Barnsdale to enforce it, instead of leaving it to the sheriffs. Until then, he would feel safer in the forest than he ever did in the valley where he had grown up.

'In any case' he would add, crossing himself with mock-seriousness, 'Our Lady Mary is there to protect me. And Mary will look after me, all right. If the stories the priests and friars tell me are all true, Mary knows what it is to be an exile on the road, with a king in pursuit, with murder in his heart and an army at his back. Ave Mary, Lady of Thieves!'.

Many in Loxley thought this was no more than one of Robin's jokes, but he was not smiling as he said it.

So Robin Hood began his career as an outlaw, and sure enough he was soon famous for his luck. He was said to be living at his ease in the forest, hunting, robbing travellers along the Great North Road—with or without the help of the Virgin Mary. He soon drew a band of kindred spirits around him.

They wore Robin's colours of green and scarlet and their names are now famous: Little John, and Much the Miller's Son, and Will Scarlock. If anyone mentioned the king to Robin in those days, Robin would say that if the king ever came to Barnsdale, he had better come wearing green and scarlet, so as not to offend the locals.

This seemingly, was another one of his jokes.

Once, Robin sent Little John, with Will Scarlock and Much the Miller's Son, to watch the Great North Road from Barnsdale Forest.

'Bring us a guest into supper,' Robin said. 'See what their appetite's like, once we've told them who we really are.'

'A guest,' John smiled. 'Right.'

'A rich guest. An earl or an abbot.'

'Right.' John said again. 'We'll bring him. And after supper.' He added, 'you can tell him all about the Virgin Mary.'

He took his bow and quiver and beckoned to Will and Much.

In the gathering dusk, from the shadow of the trees, the three thieves watched the road as it wound down the wooded escarpment towards the boggy bed of the valley of Brockadale. Before long they saw a lone knight picking his way down the hill, hurrying against the gathering chill of the evening. As he approached they saw that he was an odd sort of knight. His thinning hair was dishevelled, and his clothes and gear were patched and ragged. There were poor knights on the roads, but they were few and far between; most knights were rich men. With his rusty armour and starved-looking horse, this one seemed little more than a beggar.

'Still, he's got his own armour, so he's a knight, and he'll have to do,' John muttered.

He stepped into the road.

'Stop, friend,' he called to the knight, 'and come to supper with Robin Hood.'

The knight's eyes flickered cautiously towards the roadside. 'Supper? With Robin Hood?' he said.

There was no hiding it: the poor knight was being robbed, and he knew it. He yielded to superior force and followed the thieves quietly.

Deep in the forest, the thieves led the knight by the bridle towards the spreading shade of an ancient oak tree. From the boughs of the oak hung the bodies of the king's foresters and the Sheriff's men: those who paid the price for trying to bring Robin to book.

No sooner had the poor knight and his captors arrived, than out of the shadows, with barely the rustle of a leaf, dozens of thieves gathered, in their green and scarlet. Among them was a master thief with striking blue eyes glittering in the dark. 'Welcome stranger' he said, 'to Saint Mary's chapel.'

'Saint Mary's chapel?' the knight muttered, glancing around and up at the dead men hanging between the leaves. 'Ave Maria! It's a privilege to meet you, master Robin Hood.'

And there under the oak tree the thieves spread a white cloth and served the stranger a supper, just as sociably as if they had been in some rich man's home, for that was their custom. The knight was nonplussed, but he had no choice but to eat what was set out before him, with as good a grace as he could muster. He saw the outlaws smiling grimly, and refused to glance up again at the bodies hanging from the oak tree. He ate and drank and talked, and then patted his mouth and stood up.

'Well,' he said, as calmly as he could, 'I really must be going, gentlemen. I shall be sure to stand you all a supper,' he added, 'should I happen to pass this way again.'

'You may never come this way again,' Robin Hood said pointedly. His hand went to his knife. 'So you had best settle the bill now.'

'Oh, the bill? Me settle the bill? So that's how it is,' the knight sighed, with a glance at the glitter of the thieves' knives. 'Well friends ... if it's my money that concerns you, I'll save you the worry.'

And the knight tipped his bags on to the ground. No river of gold came flowing out. When the bags hung empty in the knight's hands, scarcely ten shillings lay on the ground.

'There's your bill. Forgive me if I don't leave a tip,' the knight said.

'Where's the rest of it?' Robin demanded.

'There is no rest of it. That's all there is,' the knight said.

'How come?'

'I have been robbed already, by worse villains than you, my thieving friends—no offence. I have been fleeced by monks.'

'Stop talking in riddles, and tell me the whole story,' Robin said. His hand remained on the hilt of his knife, and his eyes still glittered.

'If you want the whole story, you had best begin by learning my name: Richard,' said the knight. 'Sir Richard of the Lee, and I have a son. He's twenty. A year ago, he was fighting at his first tournament, and his hand slipped. Knifed a man to death. There was a fine to pay, and it wasn't a small one, as you may imagine, for a man's life. The fine was more than my son, or I, could afford to pay. So I had to borrow money. And borrow I did, from the abbot of Saint Mary's Abbey, York.'

The whole company of thieves stirred and muttered, and glanced at Robin. The knight glanced around and swallowed his surprise.

'Saint Mary's Abbey?' Robin murmured. The knight had let slip the holy name, the one thing Robin truly revered. There was a thick silence among the thieves, as the thieves hung on Robin's words.

The knight had no choice but to forge ahead with his story.

'So instead of worrying about the fine, now I worry about the loan,' he went on. 'All year I have been saving. No luck. No money. No hope of going to London to pay for lawyers, or appeal to the king. The fine's all paid, anyway, and my boy's gone across the sea now, fighting strangers, and I hear he's doing pretty well. But I'm not. The debt to the abbot falls due tomorrow, and still I've scarcely a penny to my name. 'Well,' he sighed, 'so it must be. The monks will take every acre of land that my fathers left me: the castle of the Lee, and Weardale besides. And when they have taken it,' the knight added, in a steady voice, 'I will take ship, and follow my boy, and go to Palestine, and die, and perhaps I will get more mercy from God in heaven, than ever I got from Saint Mary's monks on earth.'

He fell silent, and stared gloomily at the fire.

'Did you have no friend, willing to help?' Robin asked quietly.

'Friends? The knight gave a hollow laugh. 'A poor man with friends?'

Robin's hand was still on the haft of his knife.

'I'm lending you the money myself,' he said drily. 'Those monks have dishonoured the Virgin. They have slandered the name of Our Lady of Thieves. So Sir Richard, have the money. Have it from me, in Mary's name. Pay it me back when you can. We'll set a payment-day a year from now.'

Sir Richard glanced warily from outlaw to outlaw in the firelight. Nobody seemed to be smiling.

'Dishonoured the Virgin? Lend me the money? Are you joking?' Sir Richard asked frankly.

'I never joke.' Robin growled. 'Not about the holy Virgin.'

And he meant it. After supper was cleared away, deep in the shadows of the forest, Little John broke open a hollow tree and opened the secret hoard, counted out the glittering money into Sir Richard's saddlebags: four hundred pounds of gold. The thieves gave Sir Richard a suit of green and scarlet besides, and invited him to sleep over in the forest.

And so the evening ended, and the thieves melted away in the shadows, but Sir Richard knew that he would be watched, so he wrapped himself in his cloak and slept as best he could, under the hanging dead men, by the embers of the thieves' fire, in the place they called Saint Mary's chapel. Somehow he managed to sleep a little.

When he woke, he was alone. The birds were singing and the leaves were weaving the sunlight and the morning breeze. His horse was cropping the patchy forest turf contentedly and the embers were cold. He was alone, but his saddlebags were still stuffed with gold.

Sir Richard scratched his head. Well, he thought. Evidently I no longer need to worry about owing money to monks. I need to worry about owing money to thieves. Doesn't feel much different, really. Still, I have another year to find the money. That's progress of a sort.

He sighed and stretched.

'All I need to do now is find my way back to the road,' he muttered aloud.

'Don't worry for that,' came a deep, familiar voice. 'I'm coming with you to York.'

Sir Richard started, and turned to see the bulky form of Little John, stepping silently out of the shadowy forest.

'You can't go wandering around the forest with that kind of money,' John explained bluntly. 'There's thieves about.'

It was always hard to tell whether such things were meant as jokes.

'Besides,' John added, as if to himself, 'if I'm going to get preached at with the Virgin Mary, all day every day, I might as well go to the monks and get it done properly, in a bit of comfort. Robin can do without me for a season or two.' He caught the knight's expression, and added, 'Don't worry, Sir Richard: there is no catch. There is no trick. You will not be robbed—or not by me at any rate. Robin Hood wants you to have the money and pay back the abbot. He trusts the Virgin Mary. And it seems he trusts you. I'll make sure you get safely to York. After that, we go our own ways.'

'Then you have my word,' Sir Richard replied, 'that the money will be repaid. On time. To Robin Hood.'

John would not answer, and the two men made their way to York in silence.

5. From Silver Arrow to Silver Screen:
How the Legend of Robin Hood Adapted on Film and TV
Ashley Gregory

THE LEGEND OF ROBIN HOOD has enjoyed a century of on-screen portrayals in film and television. In 2001 Richard Clouet commented:

> The potency of the legend on the screen is revealed by a fantastic statistic, twenty-four major Robin Hood films were made in the twentieth century.

There have been over 40 film and TV productions to date (many more with references or parodies included), and the fascination continues, with two more films produced and a further one in the (re–)making since Clouet's paper.

This article compares the various versions chronologically over the decades, with reference to the journey of our legendary outlaw from the word-of-mouth musings of minstrels (medieval ballads), through literature and text, then off the page and onto the silver screen.

Robin is one of the most enduring and universally known figures of English folklore, but the story is complicated. As mentioned in previous chapters, the early ballads are medieval, dating back over 600 years. There are manuscripts dating from the 15th and 16th centuries but they are based on pre-existing material.

The ballads make many references to Barnsdale forest (the setting of several tales) and Loxley. The text is written in a northern dialect (on-screen however received pronunciation is used and much of the action takes place in Nottingham and Sherwood Forest). Robin uses violence in the ballads; representing the lower classes rebelling against those in power and for a medieval audience, brutality was the norm.

The films and TV shows are largely set during the reign of Richard the Lionheart. However, the only mention of a monarch in the early text is 'Edwarde, our comly kynge'. Despite some uncertainty, many historians point to the reign of Edward III (reigned 1327–77) as the most likely time depicted. The propensity for the film industry to use a 12th century setting is no doubt influenced by Shakespearean writer Anthony Munday (followed by 18th century antiquarian Ritson's endorsement and thanks to Sir Walter Scott's 19th century novel *Ivanhoe*). The setting, although without any real historical reference, does make for an entertaining on-screen experience and captures the audience's imagination.

There were five silent films made between 1908 and 1913 in Britain and the U.S. but *Robin Hood* (1922) starring Douglas Fairbanks arguably set the swashbuckling tone for many on-screen portrayals. This expressive silent film uses colour filters with impressive set designs. Here, Robin is known as Earl of Huntingdon (also the influence of Antony Munday) reinventing Robin as the aristocrat, (as well as setting the film during the reign of Richard the Lionheart), whereas in the ballads Robin Hood is a yeoman. The film focuses on Robin's feud between King John and Sir Guy of Gisbourne instead of the Sheriff of Nottingham. The ballad *Robin Hood and Guy of Gisburn* is the more grisly of the early ballads and includes clashes with both Gisburn and the Sheriff.

From the ballads through to the various film versions, Robin is characterised as brave, bold and heroic. In the 1922 film, the Crusades change Huntingdon as he adapts into the fearless Robin Hood, abandoning his nobility to become a highway robber and giving to the poor. Robin has an altruistic portrayal, saving the subordinates from the oppressive King John. The violence from the ballads is evident with torture scenes. Robin kills Gisbourne and joins forces with King Richard, who discovers Robin's identity, to overthrow John. The humour from the ballads is consistent throughout the on-screen versions, showing Robin's mischievousness, practical jokes and wit when faced with dangerous situations.

A noticeable inconsistency between the ballads and on-screen is the character Maid Marian. In the ballads, she doesn't exist, there are few female figures featured (the Sheriff of Nottingham's wife is one, again in one of the more humorous ballads, *Robin Hood and The Potter*) though Robin does show devotion to the Virgin Mary. In Scott's novel *Ivanhoe*, two strong female characters feature but with no romantic relation to Robin of Locksley.

The Adventures of Robin Hood (1938) has an historic reputation and became a hugely successful hit for the Warner Bros Studio, with spectacle and a fine balance between action and drama. The three-time Oscar winning film stars Errol Flynn.

This film is a loose adaptation, with some degree of fidelity to the source material from the ballads, e.g. the Sheriff's 'silver arrow' (from *The Poor Knight*) tournament features in many films and written texts, including this one. This film refers to him as Robin of Locksley, as do many later versions. He's presented as energetic, agile and youthful, with Flynn even performing some of his own stunts.

Again, the film is set during the time of Richard the Lionheart and sees an incompetent Sheriff in league with King John against Robin:

> There are some peculiarities in the film adaptations which did not exist in the medieval ballads such as the political issue of the Saxon/Norman rivalry, or the love story between Robin and Marian.
>
> *Clouet, 2001.*

The Saxon/Norman rivalry, although never mentioned in the ballads, is a touchstone of the plot in Scott's *Ivanhoe*. The character Marian features in the 1938 film.

The Oscar-winning soundtrack composed by Erich Wolfgang Korngold is a distinctive, epic and a fairy-tale-esque Hollywood score with Robin's fanfare encapsulating his heroic presence. Korngold set the tone for swashbuckling films and influenced John Williams' work on *Star Wars*.

The films and shows take liberties, but elements of the original text remain. In each version, it's forbidden to hunt deer in the forest. Barnsdale was a woodland haunt of the outlaws amongst some great expanses of royal forest. The modern understanding of the term 'forest' is of a wooded area but royal forests were simply 'preserves' and also included heaths and grassland, any areas that would support deer and game. (Forest law did apply in the Middle Ages, however Barnsdale wasn't designated a Royal Forest where deer were protected and it would have been prohibited even to carry a bow and arrow.)

Robin Hood for television differs. An honourable mention goes to Patrick Troughton, the first actor to portray Robin Hood on British TV, broadcast live in 1953. Richard Greene later took on the role in *The Adventures of Robin Hood* (1955–59). This primetime show, aimed at children, was an entertaining drama with tongue-in-cheek comedy. This production moved from studio to location filming. Producer Hannah Weinstein employed American writers who used pseudonyms due to being blacklisted (accused of supporting the Communist Party).

The theme tune by Dick James is the most enduring and recognisable, synonymous with Robin Hood and spent eight weeks in the charts in 1956. The series had many re-runs and sold to many countries across the world, possibly playing its part in ensuring the legend is so widely known and enduring.

The series has a slower pace than the films and 25–minute episodes meant only shorter stories could be told. The first episode also sees the familiar scenario of the archery tournament and briefly shows some rivalry between Will Scarlett and Robin, something that's explored in later versions.

This and further versions focus on the feud between Robin and the Sheriff, who becomes malicious in later episodes. Robin is skilled and well groomed, despite living in the forest, and his mildly altruistic side is seen again, asking for information on his target before deciding to rob Herbert of Doncaster. In this adaptation, again he's no yeoman; he adopts his nobility as a disguise to steal his possessions and gives to the poor. Locations mentioned include Doncaster, Lancaster and Collingwood, possibly referring to Collingwood Heath in South Yorkshire.

The decade of the seventies saw four films including an animation. The rom-com, *Robin and Marian* (1976) overtly plays on humour and stars Sean Connery, shaking up the formula, presenting Robin as an aging hero. Robin returns to England to reconcile with Marian following a bloody war during the Crusades. Like other versions, the Crusades changed Robin, now matured and abandoning religion, whereas Marian has converted, but they still reminisce about their times in the forest. However, Robin is resourceful, full of strength and determination as seen in his final confrontation with the Sheriff. The characters of Tuck and Scarlett imply to the viewer that many tales had been told of Robin, who had become a legend around many towns.

The film's ending loosely follows myths around Robin's death, as Little John helps him fire a final arrow on his deathbed, asking to be buried where it lands. However, in this iteration, Robin is poisoned by Marian (as opposed to being bled by a Prioress), as they both tragically die. Marian is in Kirklees, which again has some basis in folklore as the location of Robin's death, recounted in the ballads, is at Kirklees Priory. Barnsdale is also discussed as Little John wishes to return home.

Richard Carpenter (actor turned screenwriter) created the series *Robin of Sherwood* (1984–86) for a modern TV audience. *Robin of Sherwood* draws upon fantasy and an array of legends and folklore to create a quasi-mystical world. Carpenter employs an interesting take on the legend, incorporating his style and interests in mythology, legends and paganism. Herne the Hunter, whose origins also come from folklore, features as a ghostly figure. Subsequent versions have followed in this series' footsteps, such as Marian's independence and the inclusion of a 'Saracen' character.

The depiction of the Sheriff also transfers into other versions as a volatile character. Prince John's characterisation doesn't change, as his motivation is inevitably still for the throne. Marian's relationship to Richard changes; now his daughter, but as usual, Robin is instantly attracted to her. The show was hugely successful and a culmination of Carpenter's previous work including *Catweazle* (1970–71) and *Dick Turpin* (1979–82).

The second series stars Jason Connery, son of 007, as Robert of Huntingdon who becomes Robin Hood after the original Robin (Michael Praed) is killed. This plot twist stems from outlaws and criminals at times being generally referrred to as 'Robin Hood', including synonyms such as 'Robehod' and 'Robynhod' in the Middle Ages (and arguably adding to the legend). This is also seen when Herne shows Robin the future of who he will become. The phrase 'nothing is forgotten, nothing is ever forgotten' is repeated throughout the show, as Connery takes up the mantle. The ethereal theme by Celtic band Clannad added to the mystical quality of both series.

In the second iteration Robin is younger, on the cusp of adulthood, so a younger audience could identify with him, but his band of outlaws is smaller due to the budget. The show had a run-in with the infamous Mary Whitehouse, complaining it was too satanic and violent for children. The show was axed before the story finished, but Carpenter would have favoured tragedy over the more usual Hollywood-style endings; we would've seen Robin and his friends killed. Carpenter argues this over a Hollywood ending as "life isn't like that ... the whole thing [the show] has a built-in tragic theme, that you just can't fight the big boys and win."

Several high profile feature films followed in the 1990s. *Robin Hood: Prince of Thieves* (1991) stars Kevin Costner alongside a high-profile cast. This film changes the formula again as Azeem replaces Little John as Robin's sidekick, presenting a new dynamic. Female representation becomes stronger here as Marian is a fighter.

Marian and Robin have a history, being childhood friends rather than lovers. She's also now the cousin of King Richard (with a cameo by Sean Connery). A consistency in these films is Richard's arrival in the forest, which echoes King Edward's sudden appearance in the ballads.

The music is a triumphant and epic score composed by Michael Kamen. Bryan Adams' theme song for the film topped the charts for sixteen weeks and was nominated for an Oscar for Best Original Song.

This film shows Loxley castle, belonging to Robin's father. Loxley didn't have a castle (though Scott's novel *Ivanhoe* does feature Conisbrough Castle), but this backstory had not been explored before on-screen. There is some reference in that the ballads say that Robin killed his stepfather. Robin returns to his religious roots and even adopts an American accent, but he is again brave, humorous and heroic. Like previous film versions, the Crusades affect Robin, not wanting to kill unless necessary. The film also includes mystical elements, with a seer using witchcraft and a fear of evil spirits in Sherwood Forest.

Robin encounters Little John as they fight across a river and discover a bunch of outlaws, quickly becoming their leader and training them to fight, another common feature of these versions. Similarly, Robin rejects his nobility as he turns to crime as a highway robber and becoming a saviour of the people. The Sheriff states that Sherwood is the only route to London, a prime target for thieves. Friar Tuck's representation is sometimes seen as Robin's friend or his foe. Like Marian, he is a later addition to the Robin Hood tales, but nevertheless, he joins the outlaws in each on-screen version. Robin's relationship with Will changes too as it's revealed they're half-brothers.

Robin Hood (2018) is the most recent version, made for a mainstream audience with a faster pace and more action than drama. The film changes the traditional narrative of Robin Hood and plays on the contradictions of the legend, as Tuck can't remember the year. The score composed by Joseph Trapanese gives a bold and exciting motif for Robin.

Robin is called Rob and despises the rich and powerful. Rob has the same qualities as previous iterations—and rebels, setting prisoners free during the Crusades, causing hostility between him and Gisbourne. Rob returns home to find Loxley Manor in ruins and Marian in a relationship with Will. Marian's depiction dilutes her origins, as she's now a thief, who encounters Rob by stealing from him.

Little John is a Saracen and trains Rob to be the master thief. The 'Hood' is a nickname given to him, due to leaving hoods around Nottingham. Rob reveals his identity to everyone to unite people and uses Loxley Manor as a base. As a result, everyone dons hoods, protecting Rob and as a symbol of hope.

Instead of King John, an Archdeacon pulls the strings. A narrative twist sees him and the aggressive Sheriff plotting to rule, who's also given a backstory. A consistency of these films is that there's always a battle in the 3rd act. The film's ending sees a change to Will's characterisation, as he becomes Sheriff, turned against Robin through jealousy over Marian.

The various versions and accounts of Robin continue to evolve over time—transformed by folklore over many centuries and, from the 20th century, equally popular on-screen. The one constant is that Robin has proved a timeless hero with a universal appeal and the legend continues to develop for future generations. He will however retain his roots in the Sheffield suburb of Loxley.

Ashley Gregory
Sensoria/Sheffield Hallam University

ACKNOWLEDGEMENTS:
A special thanks to Jo Wingate, David X Brunt, Martin Carter, Shelley O'Brien and Dr David Clarke for their help and support in researching and writing this article.

REFERENCES AND FURTHER READING:

Bull, J. (2016). *Nothing is Forgotten: Robin of Sherwood.*

Clouet R. (2002). *The Robin Hood legend and its cultural adaptation for the film industry: comparing literary sources with filmic representations.* Retrieved from https://medium.com/lapsed-historian/nothing-is-forgotten-robin-of-sherwood-e237774d78fb

Horton, C. (2015). *From World War to Star Wars: The Music.* The Star Wars Official Website. Retrieved from https://www.starwars.com/news/from-world-war-to-star-wars-the-music

Ibeji, M. (2011). *Robin Hood and his Historical Context.* BBC History. Retrieved from https://www.bbc.co.uk/history/british/middle_ages/robin_01.shtml

IMDb. (2019). *Robin of Sherwood: Trivia.* Retrieved from https://www.imdb.com/title/tt0086791/trivia?ref_=tt_trv_trv

J. Rubén Valdés Miyares. (2019). *Who was the real Robin Hood?* Retrieved from https://www.nationalgeographic.com/archaeology-and-history/magazine/2019/01-02/origins-of-england-folk-lore-robin-hood/

Leitch, T. (2008). *Adaptations without sources: The Adventures of Robin Hood.* Literature/Film Quarterly, 36(1), 21-30.

Kennedy, M. (2007). *Robin Hood's greenwood under threat as ancient trees die off.* The Guardian. Retrieved from https://www.theguardian.com/environment/2007/oct/15/conservation

McGown, A. (2019). *The Adventures of Robin Hood.* Screenonline. Retrieved from http://www.screenonline.org.uk/tv/id/532815/index.html

Mowis, I. S. (2019). *Richard Carpenter: Biography.* IMDb. Retrieved from https://www.imdb.com/name/nm0139441/bio?ref_=nm_ov_bio_sm

Revolvy. (2019). *Hanna Weinstein.* Retrieved from https://www.revolvy.com/page/Hannah-Weinstein?cr=1

Rampell, E. (2007). *An American 'communist' in London.* The Guardian. Retrieved from https://www.theguardian.com/film/2007/nov/22/1

Schofield, C. (2018). *Why Robin Hood is a true Yorkshire hero—and not a Nottingham myth.* The Yorkshire Post. Retrieved from https://www.yorkshirepost.co.uk/news/analysis/why-robin-hood-is-a-true-yorkshire-hero-and-not-a-nottingham-myth-1-9060434

Loxley. Wikipedia: https://en.wikipedia.org/wiki/Loxley,_South_Yorkshire

Barnsdale. Wikipedia: https://en.wikipedia.org/wiki/Barnsdale